P9-CQL-403

E McB
c.1
McBratney, Sam.

I'm sorry /

2000.   11-01

HA

CASS COUNTY PUBLIC LIBRARY
400 E MECHANIC
HARRISONVILLE, MO 64701

I'm Sorry

For Dylan and Megan
–J.E.

I'm Sorry
Text copyright © 2000 by Sam McBratney
Illustrations copyright © 2000 by Jennifer Eachus
Printed in Hong Kong. All rights reserved.
http://www.harperchildrens.com
ISBN 0-06-028686-5
Library of Congress catalog card number: 99-60933
3   4   5   6   7   8   9   10
❖
First American Edition
First published in the United Kingdom by HarperCollins Publishers Ltd., 2000

I'm Sorry

Sam McBratney

Illustrations by Jennifer Eachus

0 0022 0228603 1

HarperCollins*Publishers*

CASS COUNTY PUBLIC LIBRARY
400 E MECHANIC
HARRISONVILLE, MO 64701

HA

I have a friend I love the best.

She plays at my house every day,
or else I play at hers.

I have a friend I love the best.
I think she's nice.

The things we do
always make me laugh,
and she thinks I'm nice, too.

She lets me be the teacher
when we teach our
toys to read . . .

. . . I let her be the doctor
and fix my broken bones.

We make her baby smile
when he wakes up from his nap . . .

. . . and sometimes
we put our rain boots on

to see how deep
the puddles are.

I have a friend I love the best.
I think she's nice,

and she thinks I'm nice, too.
The things we do always make me laugh.
But . . .

I SHOUTED at my friend today,

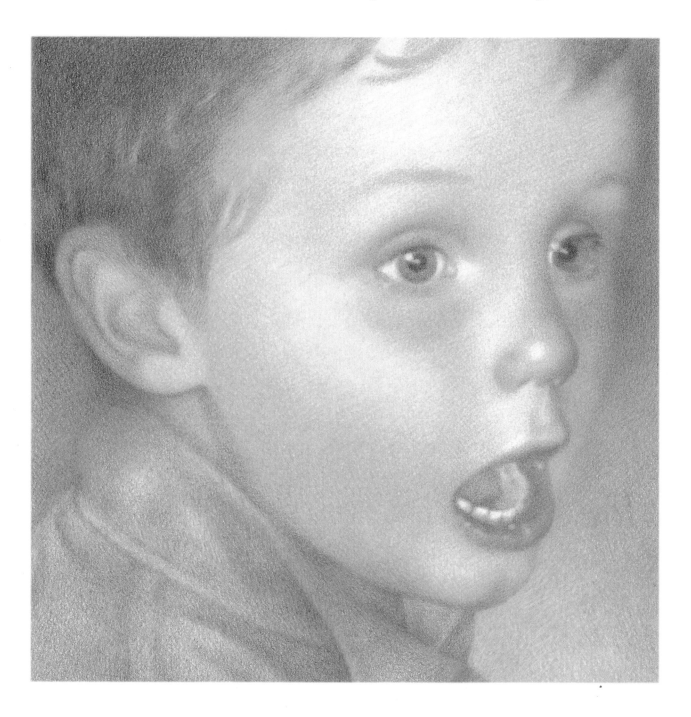

and she SHOUTED back at me.

I wouldn't speak to
her anymore, and she
wouldn't speak to me.

My friend shouted at me today,
and I shouted back at her.

She won't play with me anymore,
and I won't play with her.

I pretend my friend's not there,

and she pretends she doesn't care, but . . .

I do care.

If my friend were as
sad as I am sad, this
is what she would do:

She would come and say, "I'm sorry,"

and I would say sorry, too.